WHERE IS

Remi?

ETERNAL LOVE &
MEMORIES

KAREN DUMAS

© Copyright 2024 Karen Dumas.

All rights reserved. No part of this publication may be reproduced, stored in a retrieval system, or transmitted, in any form or by any means, electronic, mechanical, photocopying, recording, or otherwise, without the written prior permission of the author.

Order this book online at www.trafford.com
or email orders@trafford.com

Most Trafford titles are also available at major online book retailers.

Trafford PUBLISHING® www.trafford.com
North America & international
toll-free: 844 688 6899 (USA & Canada)
fax: 812 355 4082

Our mission is to efficiently provide the world's finest, most comprehensive book publishing service, enabling every author to experience success. To find out how to publish your book, your way, and have it available worldwide, visit us online at www.trafford.com

Because of the dynamic nature of the Internet, any web addresses or links contained in this book may have changed since publication and may no longer be valid. The views expressed in this work are solely those of the author and do not necessarily reflect the views of the publisher, and the publisher hereby disclaims any responsibility for them.

Any people depicted in stock imagery provided by Getty Images are models, and such images are being used for illustrative purposes only.
Certain stock imagery © Getty Images.

ISBN: 978-1-6987-1686-2 (sc)
ISBN: 978-1-6987-1687-9 (hc)
ISBN: 978-1-6987-1688-6 (e)

Library of Congress Control Number: 2024907658

Print information available on the last page.

Trafford rev. 05/21/2024

This book is dedicated to those left with paw prints on their hearts. For those who helped care for Remi in her best of times—and her trying ones too. I hope this offers some insight into the void left by the death of a pet's passing as we seek to find comfort in the love they left behind.

December 23, 2013-June 19, 2022

CONTENTS

INTRODUCTION

The first comment we make when we encounter each other in this house is, "Where is Remi?" It dictated whether the door was left opened or closed; if we needed to turn on the air to keep her cool; or just to know where she was in the yard or house. I still find myself asking, "Where is Remi?"

I want my dog and am wrangling with the harsh reality that nothing I can do will bring her back. Death is so final. Pain from the loss feels eternal.

Sure, many suggest getting another dog shortly after, but that seems … odd and unrealistic to me. Remington is irreplaceable, and having another dog attempt to fill her space feels unfair to the new dog. It sets unrealistic expectations.

So that is not my suggestion, although I encourage you to do what works for you. There are a high number of dogs in need of a home. That is how we found Remi. But for now, and for me, I want to tell Remi's story, share who she was, what she did, and how her death has left me nothing less than emotionally devastated.

The hurt I'm experiencing is almost embarrassing. Everywhere I turn, I see something that reminds me of her—a place she should be sitting or lying, things I'd buy for her, or thing we'd share. I've lost friends and family, but this is a different kind of hurt. I don't know what to do.

Writing this is cathartic for me, and hopefully, reading it will be the same for many others who have lost their fur babies.

Thank you for taking a chance on me and this book. I decided to write it after I realized there was nothing out there to help me get through the loss of my dog. But after posting about her death, I received more than 1,000 thousand likes and comments and realized I was not alone. Dogs are more than pets. They are family, friends, and confidants. And they occupy a space in our lives, homes, and hearts that cannot be refilled.

A Shepard Husky with Funny-Colored Eyes

My children were given a dog at an age when they weren't quite ready for one. I adopted him from the local humane society, and we named him Nic. A spunky puppy, he immediately took to my son. They were mutually protective of each other. However, the kids didn't respond to him responsibly, as you must do more than play with a new puppy. So I decided to teach them a lesson. I returned the dog after paying fees, immunizations, and everything else. I was making a point.

They got the point, and I returned the next day to readopt him. In that short period of time, someone else had taken a liking to Nic and adopted him. How?! It had been less than twenty-four hours! I had the representative call the lady who adopted him and offer to reimburse her and pay for another new dog. She refused, citing her attachment to the dog.

My son never forgave or forgot about this, but time and life went on. Several years later, he was speaking with my sister, Carmen—an avid and lifelong dog lover—about a dog.

He mentioned it to me, and I said sure. If you find the one you are looking for, we can get him. He was specific in his request, saying he wanted a shepherd-husky mix with funny-colored eyes. Sure. Find such an animal, and we'll get him or her. I could finally redeem myself from Nic.

Leave it to my sister to locate such a specific breed and honed request.

OUR PUP IN PORTAGE

The adoption listing was posted on www.rescueme.org and included pictures of this adorable dog named Remington. She was one and a half years old and a beautiful mix of shepherd and husky. Oh and her eyes! They were piecing and energetic. She had a personality that radiated from the pictures.

The owners were a young couple planning to move and could no longer take care of her. They desperately wanted to find her a new home and avert a shelter where she might not make it out alive.

I emailed the young lady—Madi—and told her we were interested. We scheduled a time and drove to Portage, Michigan, to get her. Portage is about two hours from our home in Detroit. We didn't know what to expect or how to prepare, but we were committed to figuring it out.

When we met the couple and Remi for the first time, she immediately took to my son. They wandered off in the park, casual and comfortable. The young lady said she'd never seen Remi take to anyone so quickly. The bond was secured.

She was comfortable knowing that Remi was in good hands, and we were sold. We paid her a hundred dollars and put Remi into the truck to go home.

The ride was quiet. Remi seemed unsure about where she was going and why.

ADJUSTING TO A NEW HOME

Having grown up with dogs, I thought I knew—or remembered—what it took to have one. We weren't sure if we needed a kennel, to let her run loose in the yard, or what. We had purchased an in-yard kennel, but that immediately proved to be too small and confining for her.

She was getting used to us and us to her. For weeks, she didn't bark at anybody or anything. She was friendly but standoffish in a snobby kind of way, but I attributed it to her acclamation and remained patient.

There were times she had to be left at home alone, and we let her have the run of the house. She was housebroken, but she clearly had to entertain herself. Hopping on the white pieces of furniture and tearing up a few items appeared to be her entertainment of choice.

Her eyes, while beautiful, were bewitching. Especially at night, they were a bit unnerving.

She also had a thing for bags. When I pulled into the driveway and exited my vehicle, she attacked any bag I was carrying.

So we went about our way of figuring her out as much as she apparently was doing the same for us.

JUST US

My son and daughter were home from school and soon returned to their respective campuses in other states. That left Remi with me. While she eventually grew on him, my husband was not a dog person, although he attempted to become one.

Either way, Remi became my road dog, literally. A gorgeous dog, she would proudly sit in the passenger set of my car and accompany me on short trips or rides. Or we'd walk around the neighborhood and attract compliments on her beauty, her eyes, her demeanor. Just her.

BACK TOGETHER AGAIN

Remi's connection with my son only got stronger, despite him not being around daily. The mere mention of his name made her ears perk up, and the sound of his car pulling into the driveway garnered her attention. Even while she and I were on walks, if she heard music coming from a car, she immediately thought it was him and would stop to look. I would calmly tell her that it wasn't Jason and to keep walking. If ever anyone could be loved the way Remi loved Jason, that would be ideal.

Jason returned to Detroit and moved into a nearby apartment. Remi visited him frequently, as he did with her at the house. He enjoyed walking, and together he and Remi would go through the neighborhood, sometimes for hours. It was their thing.

THINGS CHANGE

Twenty-eighteen was a trying year, even without realizing it was leading up to a change in how we all lived. What society viewed as normal was coming to an end. I was in a car accident I am still wrangling with residual effects from, and my daughter suddenly lost her best friend to a stroke.

Always the strong one, I found myself weakened physically and emotionally. I had to be there to provide support for my daughter and my family, but it was hard. I saw my body change in ways that made it difficult to navigate my daily tasks. Wondering what was happening and why, Remi offered a grounding that I didn't realize I needed.

My daughter Kirby had moved back home from LA, and she elevated our focus and care for Remi. She researched and bought the best of everything to ensure that Remi wasn't subjected to the same ills many of us as humans are—victims of poor food and unhealthy choices.

REGROUPING

The pandemic changed everything, and we all found ourselves back home and regrouping. It was a nice but different change of pace, with music and noises around the house I had come to miss.

The world was working from home and so were we. Technology allowed for real-time and seemingly in-person connections to take care of business, or at least as much as the shutdown and social distancing would allow. For me, it was a much needed restart, a time to reassess, recover, and refocus.

Many of my Zoom meetings were conducted with Remi at my feet. She was comforted and comforting. She'd lie on my feet, and I'd gently stroke her back to keep her settled.

Looking back, it also allowed much-needed and laser-focused time with Remi. She was the center of our existence, with her presence and needs dictating every decision, purchase, and move. It sounds crazy, but it was true. We never left her alone at home, and Kirby expanded every aspect of Remi's existence. That expansion included her having the run of the house and furniture. She was at home and acted like it.

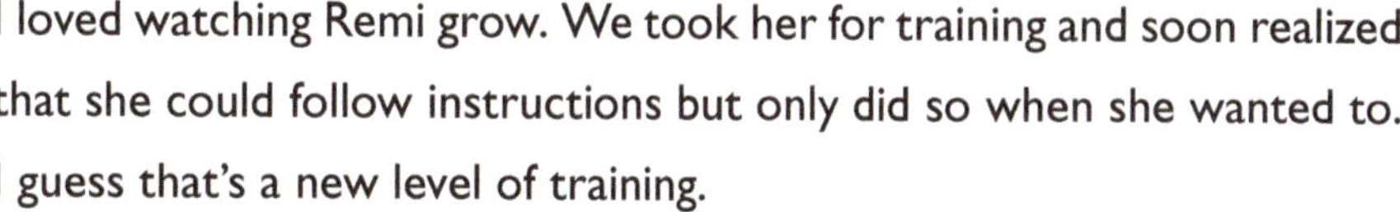

I loved watching Remi grow. We took her for training and soon realized that she could follow instructions but only did so when she wanted to. I guess that's a new level of training.

She looked quite intimidating and barked when anyone approached. I knew she was fierce and would tap into her protective mode if provoked. That was enough for me.

Winters were her favorite. She would play in the snow or sit atop the patio table as a queen would on her thrown. I loved watching her play in the snow or sit and watch out of the window at the snowfall. I still expect to see her playing in the snow.

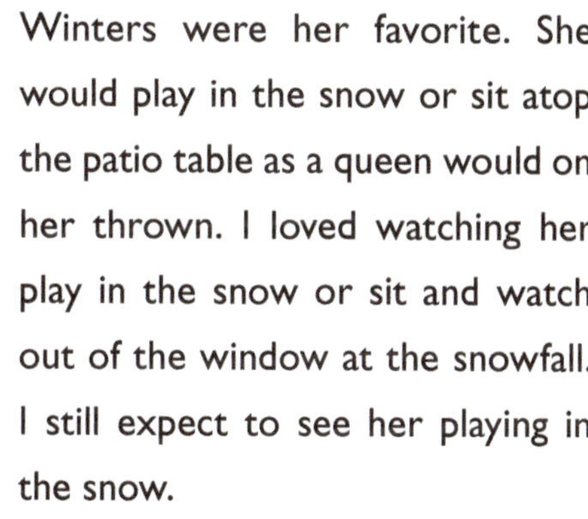

REMI DAYS

The following two years were filled with Remi. Really. It was her world, and looking back, I regret nothing. As I write this, I still cannot believe she is gone. I expect to see her walking through the hall, lying on her chair, or cuddled up in either Jason or Kirby's spaces.

While shopping one day, I saw a fabulous round chair on a rotating base. It had a large, round cushion and looked perfect for Remi to lie on in the kitchen. We needed something after she took over the two overstuffed chairs, which had to be reupholstered from her wear.

My son and I rented a U-Haul to get the chair from Home Goods. The sales rep complimented us on the purchase and was shocked when I told him it was for our dog. But it was. And she loved it. We kept it covered to keep its light color clean and had pillows for her comfort. It was also the place where she hid her treats or toys she wanted to revisit later.

The chair remains in the kitchen, with her cover and pillows. I still expect to see her lying there whenever I walk by.

My shopping trips always included toys and balls for her, neither of which lasted long.

We celebrated her birthday, prepared her filets, and gave her bottled water. Nothing but what we thought was best for her. Always.

HOW LONG IS FOREVER?

I was never so naive that I thought Remi would be around forever. But I never thought she would be cheated of what I had hoped would be a long life. I would sometimes google her breed to see her life expectancy, knowing that it was not up to any of us how long she—or we—would live. I just didn't think it would be so soon.

I feel as though she was cheated. And so were we.

HER PAW

I don't know if any of this had anything to do with her demise, but my mind constantly goes back over everything as I wonder what happened, and if I could have done anything different.

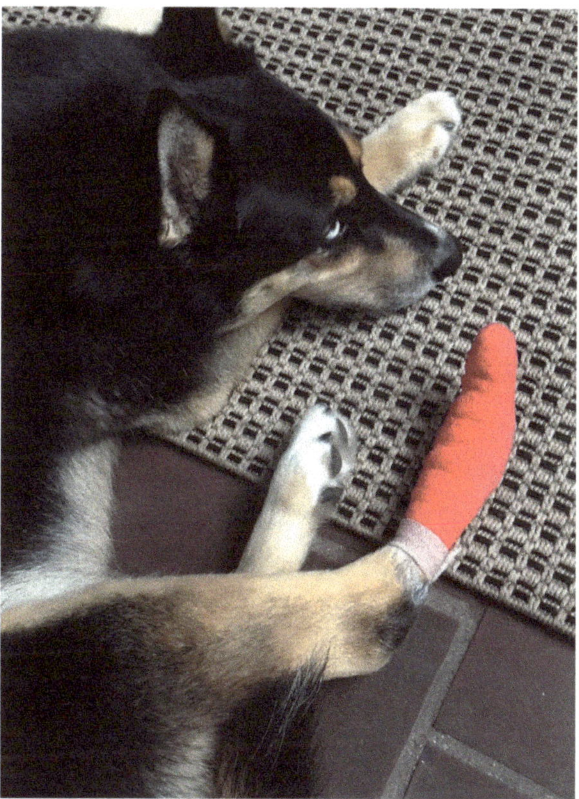

The groomer cut her toenail too short, and it became irritated. We took her to the vet, who prescribed an antibiotic. She later seemed to be limping a little, although she hadn't fallen or suffered any injury. We took her back twice when it didn't seem to improve, each time she was given medicine.

HER STOMACH

Thereafter, she began having digestive issues. She wouldn't eat. This was unusual for her, and we watched her closely and began trying all kinds of options to get her to eat. Two subsequent visits to her vet indicated we needed an ultrasound to identify if there were any issues that we should be aware of.

She was clearly struggling to go to the bathroom and less energetic from not eating.

We took her to a local hospital that could provide an ultrasound.

THE HOSPITAL

The veterinary hospital rivaled that of an urgent care for humans. The facility, the options, and the costs were beyond what one would expect for pets. They had veterinary specialists ranging from internists to oncologists to cardiologists. What they lacked was a level of compassion that we were accustomed to from her vet, Platz, in Grosse Pointe, Michigan.

This place, while professional, was quite robotic in its service. It felt very clinical and detached. The focus was on cost, not care or compassion.

On her first visit, they took her back for the exam and hospitalized her. The ultrasound showed that she had gastrointestinal lymphoma. Four days and nearly ten-thousand dollars later, we checked her out knowing she didn't want to be there and that it wasn't in her best interest.

They'd send a nightly photo of Remi. She was in what appeared to be a cold and tiled area. While it was probably best and provided an ease of care for the animals, it was not Remi's vibe. It was evident in her eyes that she didn't want to be there. We brought her home.

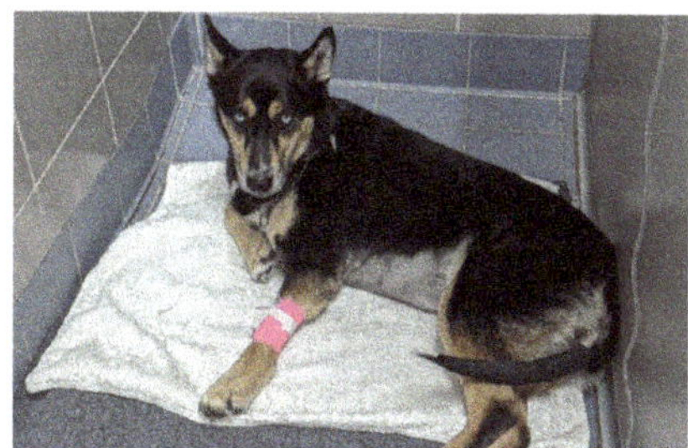

They said gastrointestinal lymphoma was treatable but not curable. We wanted her to be as comfortable as possible. That meant she had to be home, where she was most comfortable and cared for.

Every visit back for the scheduled therapy was expensive and stressful; we reassured her we were not going to leave her there, and we didn't. But it was where we had to take her the morning she died.

The days that followed were different than those generally shared with Remi. She was becoming a reduced version of herself.

The medicine offered temporary hope as we saw some signs of improvement in her appetite and digestion. We had hope.

But often with loved ones, people prop them up for selfish reasons, not taking into consideration what's best for them. I didn't want that for her. I wanted her well, but I was also realistic in my expectations.

In addition to the oncologist at the hospital, we kept in touch and visited her regular vet. Dr. Gabe is an angel with a veterinary degree. His level of responsiveness and compassion are unmatched and brought a level of comfort during those stressful times. He cared, and it showed.

We also had a secondary vet come to the house, just to double-check and make sure she was getting through the tough days OK. She was not.

No excitement for toys, not begging for a bite of whatever we were having, no hopping on the stairs to signal she wanted her favorite treat from Trader Joes, no going to her toy box to pick a toy, and no excited response to the invitation for a walk.

HOW DO YOU SAY GOODBYE?

Up until the end, I hoped and prayed for a miracle. I wanted my Remi back. Instead of running to the back door when she saw us pull up, she spent her days lying by the gate rarely looking up.

We tried every food option to get her to eat, sometimes fixing several items to see if any piqued her interest. We even literally fed her by hand—whatever it took to get her the nourishment she needed.

Sometimes, she wanted to stay on the back deck at night. We allowed her to, camping out in the sunroom, the kitchen, or literally at the back door as my daughter did one night.

We were committed to giving her whatever she needed and letting her know we were there for her.

I can remember taking her for what would be our last walk. It was just around the block, but she seemed tired and struggled to finish the route. I remember her looking up at me, and I told her it was OK. Take your time, Remi. We'll get back OK.

THE SIGNS

In her own way, she was saying goodbye on the last day she was here. She went to her favorite chair and just placed her head on it. Jason helped her onto the chair, where she stayed for a brief while before making her rounds. She half-heartedly played with a toy for a moment before walking away from it. She was lying in areas she didn't usually, behind a table or behind a chair in the living room.

She spent her last day with Jason, who doted on her excessively, giving her medicine and feeding her by hand. Kirby was out for the day but joined them on her return. Rubbing Remi's belly was always a favorite and comforting for her. We did all of that.

My daughter had googled dog behavior when they are sick, and alienation was a characteristic when they were declining.

GOOD NIGHT

Kirby and Jason camped out in the sunroom. The doors remained open to give Remi fresh air, and she cuddled up on the blankets for what would be her last night.

I was awakened by my daughter telling me that Remi wasn't breathing.

I rushed downstairs to find my son cleaning where she had lost her bowels. He then wrapped her in a blanket and put her in one of her pillow cocoons.

Everyone was in tears, and we didn't know what to do. It was 3:00 a.m. on a Sunday morning. Father's Day. For human emergencies, you call 911. What were the options for pets? I called her vet and the hospital, which was our only option. We could have waited for the crematorium to open at eight, but that was five hours away.

We gently loaded her in the back of the truck and began the thirty-minute drive to the veterinary hospital in Oakland County. We were all quietly sobbing at the thought of everything we had just lost.

SO, NOW WHAT?

The morning was emerging. The world was unaware of what the night before held. We were quiet. No one knew what to say. Remi was gone.

We started gathering some of her items. We tossed her medicines, which occupied the refrigerator and counter. We removed her feeding bowls and the water bowls around the house. It wasn't that we were trying to erase her presence, but we had to remove the stark reminders of her absence.

Her chair and favorite pillows remained, as does the "Beware of Dog" signs, which hang on the wrought iron fence to the backyard. Her toy chest is still full, and her leash and collar sit atop as they always did, ready for her walks. I keep one of her toys on my bed.

I waited until the next day to text Dr. Gabe. He had generously given so much of his free time to us, I didn't want to occupy his Father's Day. I also waited before sharing on my social media. The post garnered more than a thousand reactions and was a window into the pain that so many endured when they, too, lost their pets. I wasn't looking for sympathy, but I have shared so much of Remi with others via social media that I thought they should know. And I had to get it out. The words, the tears, the hurt. Maybe that was a little of letting it go. It was—but not for long.

We packed up her many pillows and bedding, most unused, along with food, collars, treats, and other items. We took them to Detroit Animal Care. They took the items from our car and into the facility through the back door. I know it wasn't a million-dollar donation, but everything we took was special to us and Remi. The employees took the items in a very cold and unappreciated manner. Maybe it wasn't, and perhaps I was selfishly expecting more. A thank you, perhaps?

fo

WHEN IS TOMORROW?

I felt the same deep-seated void that I did when I lost my mom. It was a pain that I knew that no matter how much time passed, it would never be filled. People may not understand or agree with that statement, but that is the depth of my pain.

I took the liberty of writing my weekly column for the *Detroit News* about Remi. I almost felt guilty, given that our community and society have so many issues to deal with. I see people losing their homes, family members, jobs, etc. But I wasn't in competition with anyone or anything for whose pain, hurt, or issues were greater. I was dealing with my own.

Friends sent cards, flowers, and memorial gifts, including an etched-glass photo of Remi. I appreciate them all. They say I'll feel better soon. One day. Maybe tomorrow. Or maybe not.

It is said that time heals all wounds. That is a lie. My mom passed away more than twenty years ago and that wound remains raw. I fear the wound from Remi will remain the same.

I haven't been able to go into the backyard or sit on the deck. I expect to see Remi there, enjoying the outdoors, chasing a squirrel, playing in the pond, or posing on the deck. Going into the pantry is hard as it is where I'd peek out of the window to check on her as she sat curled by the gate. When I pull into the driveway, she isn't at the gate, the door, or looking out of the front window, where we kept the blind slightly raised so she could see out. It remains raised.

Everything reminds me of Remi. Everything.

STILL WATCHING OVER ME

Every night, I say my prayers, and I cry. Where's Remi? I've heard about the Rainbow Bridge, where pets travel after death, but that hasn't comforted me. I stare at the ceiling and wonder without questioning God's decision. And I wish. Just as I did for my mom and other loved ones who I've lost; I wish for a different outcome.

The night after we lost her, I remember staring at the ceiling. I could see a shadow that resembled Remi's profile. I thought I was seeing things. Until I saw it the next night, and I've seen it every night since. This shadow clearly outlines her nose, ears, and upper body.

I want to take a picture, but I fear it won't be visible. Maybe it's there just for me. I showed it to my daughter, and she saw it. At least she said she did. I fear rearranging anything as I don't want to lose whatever is creating that shadow. It disappears when the sun rises.

After a couple of months, it disappeared for good. I still look every night. Just shy of the first anniversary of her death, I noticed what appeared to be wet paw prints on the kitchen floor, leading to the back door. Only someone missing a loved one would believe this. I took a picture as they eventually faded away.

OUTSIDE

The backyard was always a place of comfort and peace for me and Remi. Yet it is a place I have been unable to return to for any period. I constantly stare out of the back door and look at all the places that I'd expect her—running through the yard, hiding her toys under the deck, roaming the rocks surrounding the pond, or sitting at the gate and gazing at the cars or people walking down the street.

I often wondered if she longed to be free. I guess she is now.

We rebuilt the back deck, and many of her hidden toys were found under the porch. I asked the contractors to save them for me. I'll keep those too.

As summer ends and the snow will soon begin to fall, it will serve as yet another reminder of her absence. She loved the snow and looked regal in it.

IT'S ALL SO FINAL

I've always been the person with solutions—contacts, resources, ideas, and energy to solve nearly every problem encountered. But I can't with this one. There is no answer, no solution, and no redo. No amount of love or tears can bring Remi back to me. If that were possible, she would be back.

Instead, her ashes sit on a shelf behind me with her picture atop the urn. My daughter purchased a wind chime with her name on it to hang outside, hoping that would help me return to the backyard easily and peacefully. Not yet.

Her picture frequently pops up on my social media memories, and I am reminded of the fragility of life. I had no idea that I would be writing about or mourning her loss so soon. I know it isn't up to any of us, but we like to fool ourselves into thinking we have more time than we do. We don't. She didn't, and I am forever changed as a result.

My heart has not beat the same since.

Remington

ACKNOWLEDGMENTS

While this is my second published work, this is by far my most personal and emotional. It would not have been possible without the love and support of my family and those who continue to uplift, support, and encourage me to follow my dreams and execute my ideas.

Dr. Curtis L. Ivery has been a longtime supporter and mentor, always encouraging excellence and the pursuit of something greater. Dr. Micky Golden Moore, who was introduced to me from George Jackson, has been a wealth of grief support. Her book and social media group, Beyond the Pawprint, has been a safe and nonjudgmental space in which to grieve.

I am thankful for Dr. Gabe of Platz Veterinary Clinic in Grosse Pointe. His compassion, accessibility, responsiveness, and professionalism are unmatched.

Candace of B & B Grooming, who came to the house and provided onsite grooming for Remi and continues to check on us to this day.

To the thousands, literally, who responded to my *Detroit News* columns and social media posts. Pet grief is real. None of us are alone.

And to Remi for bringing a light to my life that will forever burn. I am sad for her absence but better for her presence.

Karen Dumas is a communications professional and media contributor committed to excellence, entrepreneurship, and equality. As founder of Images & Ideas, Inc., she has earned a reputation as an effective strategist with proven results. Dumas also served as chief of communications and external affairs for Mayor Dave Bing and the City of Detroit.

Dumas is a columnist for the *Detroit News* and covoice on the *No BS Newshour* with Charlie LeDuff. Respected as a trusted and fair radio host, television contributor, and columnist, she is known to be "honest and engaging" and has been recognized by *HOUR* magazine as "the more intelligent choice" of talk-radio show hosts.

She served on the board of directors for the Detroit Zoological Society, was the inaugural chair of the diversity and inclusion committee, and a member of the communications and marketing committee, governance and nominating committee, and the executive committee. Previously, she has served on the editorial advisory board of *BLAC* magazine, the communications committee for the Detroit Riverfront Conservancy, the board of directors for SPHINX, the PR committee for the NCAA Final Four/Detroit, board chair for the Arts League of Michigan, and the board of directors and PR committee chair for Detroit PAL (Police Athletic League), among many others. The City of Detroit, the State of Michigan, Real Times Media, and several Who's Who entities have recognized her achievements.

Dumas is a frequent guest speaker at schools and professional organizations seeking insight into performance-based practices, the tools for success, living, and treating others with fairness, women's challenges in the workplace, and balancing professional and personal roles. A frequent event moderator and mistress of ceremonies, her professional but entertaining demeanor enhances any event or organized gathering; her presentations are informative and inspirational for all.

She is also a regular guest contributor for FOX2 and other media outlets.

www.karendumas.com

Printed in the USA
CPSIA information can be obtained
at www.ICGtesting.com
LVHW060043090624
782672LV00018B/220